Dedication

Parkville High is dedicated to everyone; to all who live with different disabilities, their families, and their friends. This book is dedicated to people who don't understand different disabilities and feel the need to make fun of, or have pity for the disabled population. This is a story that will relay the message that people are all the same. We all experience different trials and tribulations in life, and we share the same dreams, thoughts, feelings, and fears. Hopefully this book will entertain and enlighten its readers.

I want to thank all of the people that have inspired me to write Parkville High.

FAMILY/FRIENDS

My wife to be Danielle and my Princess Skylar, you two motivate and inspire me to do great things. Love you!

JOBS

Board of Child Care (Baltimore, Maryland)
I worked as a child care worker from 2003-2005. I learned the value of patience, and I saw how powerful it is to love people, and to put other people's needs ahead of your own. I give thanks to Nygera for referring me, and I thank you John Charton for hiring me. Thanks to all of my great co workers and of course the kids. Mr. H loves you, no cursing!

Independent Living Association (Brooklyn, New York)
I supervised a facility for the developmentally disabled from 2005-Present. I truly learned that people are all the same while working here. My brother Q, thank you for referring me. Stephanie Mays, thank you for hiring me, and always encouraging and believing in me. Thanks to my co workers and of course my Individuals. Love you ALL!

Special Thanks to Derick Cross, Tracy Dunne-Derrell, and Heather Watkins for sharing my vision!

PARKVILLE HIGH

Written by: Heddrick M. McBride

Illustrated by: Derick Cross

Edited by: Tracy Dunne-Derrell
And
Lystra A. Lessey

Table of Contents

Prologue

The crowd is singing along with the band "I Believe I Can Fly, I believe I can touch the sky." The lights from the cameras are flashing brightly. All of the graduates are marching one by one with perfect timing. It is only standing room; there is not an empty seat in the building. My proud mother is seated in the front row with a big smile on her beautiful face. My cap is placed perfectly, and my gown is falling just right over my new suit. I'm Arthur Thomas, and this is exactly how I thought my high school graduation would be. I never would have imagined that I, Party Artie, from Harlem New York, would have to come to Charlotte, North Carolina to see this great day come true. I remember it all just like it was yesterday. What a crazy year this has been for me, my mother, and my crew.

Chapter One- Summertime on the Block; August 15, 2011

It started off as a regular summer night on my block, 123rd Street between 7th and 8th Avenues. It was about 5:30pm, and my best friend Anthony Evans, aka Big Tone, just yelled outside my window for me to come downstairs. Tone was one of the biggest, toughest, seventeen-year-old kids that you ever met. He stood 6 feet 2 inches and was 220 pounds of pure muscle. Ranked number one out of all junior football players last season, he has at least 50 letters from colleges all over the country who want him. The funny thing about Tone was that even though he was tough as nails, he was a "pretty boy." Tone was brown skinned and had light brown eyes, so all of the ladies on the block and in his school loved him. I always told him that he was too pretty to be so tough.

Tone has been my best friend since the 3rd grade. We met at a fireman's family appreciation dinner. Both of our dads were firemen who were stationed at Firehouse 45 in the Bronx.

"Artie put some air in your wheels and come downstairs. I know you probably caught a flat, chasing after Tasha all day." Tone always had jokes; he was talking about my wheelchair. For most of my life, I have been a wheel chair user, due to a condition called muscular dystrophy. I still have feeling in my legs, but they are not strong enough for me to stand up on my own for long periods. I was walking normal until I reached the age of six. Gradually, the muscles in my legs got weaker, and I needed my chair ever since. The only time I can stand up for long is if I hear some Mary J Blige or some good "old school" music. That's when I hit them with the famous Artie Two Step!

"Chill out Block Head," I yelled out of my window. "I'll be down in a minute."

It's a good thing that my building had an elevator and a ramp outside, so I always got outside with no problems. When we had that blizzard last winter, I had to keep a small shovel with me at all times, just to leave the building.

"What's good Big Tone, I'm hungry, are you trying to grab a bite? I am tired of the same old food; I want something good to eat."

He said, "I hear that my man, do you have any real money? Because all I have is thirty bucks on me."

"I have twenty on me, but you know there is always a way brother. Why don't you sing a love song to one of these ladies out here, lover man? I'm sure that could get us at least ten more dollars. "

"Ah, you are a funny dude, Artie. I just saw Chubby Charles up the block, and if you are feeling good, then we can double our money." He didn't have to say another word, because Tone and I always knew what each other were thinking. Chubby Charles came from a family of hustlers, so he was interested in anything connected to making money. Charles was about 5 feet 6 inches tall and at least 230 pounds. He was a light skinned dude, so we sometime called him Heavy C, after the legendary rapper Heavy D. He was only nineteen years old, but you could find him at every dice game or gambling spot in Harlem.

"Chubby C," Tone yelled, "I got fifty ones in my pocket that say that my man Party Artie will dust you in a race from here to the corner."

Charles laughed for a second. "Artie has skills with that chair, but he definitely doesn't want to see me. But I will gladly take your pocket money, so let's do it, Big Fella."

Whenever Tone got into a discussion or argument with anyone, he always clapped his big hands together while he talked, and got very loud. As he started clapping those huge hands he yelled, "Charles, you must be bugging if you think you can beat my man. Start stretching now, because it's going down."

At this point, everyone who was outside came over to see what the commotion was about. Cool Lou came by with his radio in hand to see what was going on. At twenty-one years old, he loved to be in the middle of everything. He came by with his big radio blasting 50 Cent's classic, *I Get Money*, so now everyone on the block was singing, dancing, yelling, and laughing. I saw a few people on the side making side bets of their own.

I leaned to my man. "Tone, you might as well start making reservations for dinner, because Chubby C is treating." Then I yelled out, "Chubbs, I will keep it close, so that you don't look too badly out here."

As he reached out to shake my hand, Charles laughed, "I hope your chair is oiled up, my Dude, don't want your wheels to lock up on you." I shook his hand, and said, "No doubt, big man, just make sure you don't pay us with change, because we like the kind of money that folds."

Cool Lou went to the end of the block to serve as the judge and finish line. Whoever got to him first would be the winner. If you know Harlem, then you know how long our blocks are, so we started from the middle of the block. Tone yelled, "ON YOUR MARKS, GET SET, AND GO!"

I got off to a fast start, but surprisingly Charles was right with me stride for stride. After about fifty feet Charles slowed down, and then eventually stopped running, as he watched me glide to the finish line twenty seconds later. The block was filled with people clapping and laughing at the whole scene and of course laughing at Charles. Lou, who was holding the money, gave me the hundred bucks and gave me an extra $20 that came from the side bets that he had made on me. Big Tone came over and we did our special hand shake. "That's my man," he said "Easy does it."

We couldn't have planned it any better, because as soon as he said that, Maria and Bianca, two fine Puerto Rican girls from the next block walked over and said, "Nice race Arthur."

I have always had a thing for Maria. She was my age, average height with a light brown complexion, and some long wavy hair that I loved. Not to mention that she was full of curves and had a beautiful smile. Her cousin Bianca was hot too; same height, a little bit darker with a pretty long pony tail. She had the same curves and pretty smile that must run in their family. She was a year older than us, but we have known them both for years. I grabbed Maria's hand. "Thanks Mami, do you and Bianca want to come get some Arroz con Pollo with me and my Big Man?"

Bianca looked at Tone and quickly said, "Maria can I talk to you for a minute?" They talked for about 20 seconds, and then Maria came back. "Sure, we will join you guys for a bite to eat." Me and Tone winked at each other and headed towards the Cuban restaurant on Fifth Avenue with the ladies. Before we could get off of the block, I got a text message from my Moms.

Come home right away, we need to talk!

13

I called Moms right away, "Moms, what's up are you good?"

"Of course son, but I need to speak with you right away, so start heading home right now." As much as I hated to leave my man hanging and miss out on a great date, Moms came first. I pulled Tone to the side.

" Moms needs me at the crib, so I have to be out. I will come outside later on."

"Handle your business playboy; call me later if you need me."

I turned to our dates "Ladies, I have an emergency, so can we get a rain check on this date?" Maria told me to call her later and kissed me on my cheek, so hopefully I didn't blow it all together. I rushed home to see if everything was ok with my mother.

Chapter Two- Carolina Bound

I got home as fast as I could; it had to be something important for my Moms to call me like that. My Mother, Paula Thomas, was petite, but she was no joke. She was brown skinned, with beautiful brown eyes, and soft, curly shoulder length hair. My Dad always called her the "Queen of Sheba," whatever that means. He always said, "Your mother looks sweet and gentle as a lamb, but she is as tough as a tiger! Always listen to her, and respect her as our Queen."

She always showed she could handle herself in any situation, so giving me an emergency call concerned me. Moms worked as manager at Bank of America, so she was respected in the neighborhood. Every single man, and even some married men have tried to hit on my Moms. She quickly shut them down and made sure they apologized after trying. Of course I never witnessed any of this, but Cool Lou always kept us up on the current events of the neighborhood.

My Pops died three years ago while working on a routine fire in the Bronx. He and Tone's Pops, Mr. Evans, were on duty on the night that a ten-year-old boy decided to experiment with his older brother's cigarettes in his bedroom. He thought that his grandmother was coming, so he threw the cigarette into the trash can in his room. I often think back to that day, "He could have at least put the cigarette out, and maybe my Pops would still be here." Mr. Evans got in there, and got the boy's little sister and her cat out of the blaze. Mr. Evans told us that my Pops got the boy and his grandmother out of the apartment, but he went back to make sure that there weren't anymore potential victims in the house. By the time he went back in, the smoke had become too much for him to handle. By the end of that evening, all of the occupants of the apartment were safe at a designated location; The Prince and the Queen were without their King forever.

My Dad was 6 feet 4 inches, but it seemed like he was 8 feet tall. Pops was full of muscles, but he treated everyone very gently. He always wanted to make sure that everyone was comfortable and happy. Pops was dark brown and had dark brown eyes that could make my body freeze when they were fixed on me. If I did something wrong, those eyes always let me know. Pops always kept a low hair cut, with a well groomed beard. Pops always took pride in his appearance, and he taught me to value looking good at a young age. "Son, always make sure that you are sharp at all times. Make sure that you look and smell good at all times."

"Okay Pops," I always said in response.

"But more importantly, make sure that that your words make you shine! Always have the right words to say in any situation. Never let anyone kill your spirit with words, or make you lose your cool. With the look and smell of success, you can tell any story that you want to."

It was 7:45pm; I went straight to the living room, expecting to see Moms watching Wheel of Fortune, one of her favorite shows. To my surprise, Moms was seated in the kitchen at the table, listening to Anita Baker's classic song "Rapture."

"Moms, what's good? Why are you in here? You must have known all of the answers, or maybe Vanna White had on an old dress tonight? Why aren't you watching the wheel?" I know Moms very well, and whatever her message was, she wanted to deliver it to me face to face. She probably wants to start talking about my college plans, or maybe the dirty clothes that I left on bedroom floor earlier when Tone called me outside.

My Mom never takes pity on me for anything. She always told me, "If you are not going to do things for yourself, then don't expect them to get done." I learned how to master this wheelchair, and use my arms, hands, feet, nose, and even my face in order to get things done. I learned how to cook, wash clothes, and sew, under Moms' watch. "Prince, I'm glad that you're here, we need to talk." My Moms is never one to beat around the bush or sugar coat things. "It is what it is" is her favorite expression. "Prince, my company offered me a position as a project manager at the Corporate Center. The only thing is it's located in Charlotte, North Carolina. The position will be open at the end of August, so I have a week to make my decision."

I laughed at first. "Move to Charlotte Moms? I know you told them that we can't move out there with the farmers. At least they tried. My Moms is the best thing that happened to that company. So what's good, you found a new job?"

"Prince, listen, I found a bigger house for me and you, and I will be making a lot more money. We will be able to put some money together for you to go to college." Even though that sounded good, I wasn't trying to hear it. "What about me? What about all of my friends? Everyone loves us here, so why would we leave?" I could tell that Moms wasn't too sure about the move, because she entertained me in an argument. She normally would shut me down, and tell me how things were going to happen.

"Son, let me tell you something, your father and I set high expectations for this family. I still have goals that I am trying to accomplish, and you are going to be a success."

"How can we leave New York, Moms? I only have one year left of school, and there is no place for the Young Prince in North Carolina. I love you to death Moms, but I'm not milking a cow for anyone. What about all of my peoples up here? I would be leaving all of my friends."

Moms regained her strength at this point. "Yeah, I thought about that. I think it would be a good idea for you to have a change of scenery. I have heard about you being around some shady people and bad situations."

I rose up in my chair. "What are you talking about Moms? Who's telling lies on me?" She eased her tone and said, "Son, it's natural for you to be attracted to the excitement of the streets. Lord knows that your father wasn't always an angel. I have too much invested in our family to let anything happen to you." I thought that I had one more strong point to make, "All of our family is either in New York or Chicago, so we will be out there by ourselves. No one will care about us out there."

A mom always has the answers to shut their kid down. "Prince, we made it in Harlem, so we can make it anywhere! We have to do what's best for us at the end of the day. People will act like they love you whether you are successful or struggling, but you better believe that life always goes on. You need to choose who you want to be, and what type of life you want to lead. You can be whatever and whoever you set out to be." As I was going back and forth with Moms, all I could see was my Pops saying, "Listen to the Queen, Son, she knows what she is talking about."

"Moms, I respect you and love you, but I'm not feeling what you are saying. I need some time alone to think," I said. I closed my eyes, expecting a smack on the back of my head, but Moms let me go outside without a fight.

As much as I love Moms and respect her opinion and guidance, I still needed reassurance. I called Big Tone to meet me at the schoolyard to talk about this situation. "Tone, what's good Man?" Moms just got a good job in North Carolina, and we may be moving out there next month. That would be crazy right?"

Tone really threw me off with his response. "That may be a good idea, Artie. It's nothing new going on in Harlem, just these same miserable people trying to come up off of each other."

I was confused at this point, "What do you mean? We get nothing but love around the way. What's wrong with staying home?"

Tone grabbed my arm. "Think about it, Artie, there is a whole world out there that we don't know about, and that doesn't know about us. We are from New York City, the best city in the world. I am a young version of L.L Cool J in his prime. If Chris Paul can have his own charity bowling tournament on ESPN, then anything is possible. Once the world meets people like us, then it's all over. I might end up with my own celebrity dice game right in front of the Apollo one day." Tone could always bring light to tough situation.

"North Carolina is deep in the country though. It will just be me and Moms, with no one else to look out for us. But never mind that, since when have you been a number one fan of North Carolina?" I knew Tone too well for the conversation to go that smoothly.

We went to the pizza shop to get a slice and a soda.

Tone finally came clean. "Between me and you A, U.N.C Tar Heels is my first choice of college teams, so I will be near you next year if you move out there. I already had this talk with my parents, and they agree that changing scenery wouldn't be a bad move for me. Artie we are making it in Harlem, so we could have the rest of the world in the palm of our hands!" I shook Tone's hand. "That's why I mess with you Block Head; you make sense when you want to. I still have to think about it. I'll see you tomorrow kid."

I took a long time getting home. I sat in front of my building for about 30 minutes, just thinking and checking out the scenery. I got home and Moms was seated in the living room going through our old family picture albums. I said "Moms, you made some good points, and you are too beautiful to say no to. I guess Carolina is the move." I went to Moms IPod and played *Never Too Much* by Luther Vandross. That was our favorite song, so I said, "Mom' let's dance to celebrate our future and to say goodbye to Harlem." Tears of joy ran down her face as she gave me a kiss on my cheek and danced with me.

"Mama knows best, boy! I'm glad that I didn't need the belt this time." We both laughed at that one and did our secret hand shake that I taught her. My Moms is something else. She is hard as a rock on the outside, but melts whenever I stare at her with my brown eyes or when we are dancing and having fun. Maybe I remind her of my Pops. She is definitely my favorite lady in the world.

We had a going away party at the house two weeks later. All of our family and friends from the neighborhood were there. Everyone wished us well and we all promised to keep in touch with one another. Tone and Mr. Evans helped us pack our last minute things. Moms' job had hired a moving company to take care of the heavy duty stuff a few days ago. Tone and I had been together since the 3rd grade, so it was pretty hard for us to say good bye. We went to the schoolyard to have one last talk before I left.

"This is it, Block Head, I'm out. Make sure you do your thing in football this year. Make sure you take care of all my ladies while I'm gone."

He laughed. "Artie, you take care and do your thing out there. Always remember that you are from Harlem, so you are always one step ahead of the game. When I come down and visit, make sure you have a few country gals for me to choose from."

I laughed too. "I got you kid." Tone shook my hand gave me a hug, and said, "I love you Bro, be good. Call me later on."

"Love you too, Bro." Even though we meant these words we looked at each other and laughed because it just sounded too corny. We went back to my building and the truck was loaded up. My Moms was parked out front in her white 2010 Range Rover. Tone helped me get in the truck, and we were off to Charlotte.

Chapter Three- Welcoming Committee

I can't lie; the house that Moms picked out for us was no joke. We had three bedrooms, two bathrooms, and front and back yards. Charlotte had the one thing that you don't have in Harlem: space. The house was one level, so I could get around to every area with no problem. It also had a ramp in the front and in the back of the house especially for me to make moves. Moms had a driveway, plus a private garage on the side of the house. We even had a fireplace, which was much different from the fire escape that we had in New York.

We had neighbors on both sides of us. The Robinsons were an elderly couple who lived on the left of us. Mr. Robinson was a retired insurance salesman, who loved fishing and working on his garden. Mrs. Robinson was a retired nurse at the local hospital who loved to bake cookies and cakes. They were very polite and friendly people. They had an older son, Rodney, who lives in Atlanta with his wife and two kids. When we first moved in, they knocked on the door an hour later to welcome us to the neighborhood. Mrs. Robinson baked us an apple pie that smelled so good. I should have known to wait, since she was wearing oven mitts to bring it over. I burned my fingers trying to eat it before it could cool off. The Robinsons told us to be careful and keep a close eye on our other neighbors, the Kelly family. Mr. Robinson said, "Me and Mabel are not racist folks, but those white people are crazy!"

Moms being concerned, said, "What's wrong with them? They don't like having black neighbors?" Mr. Robinson said, "They play loud music, they break things, they fight, they fuss, they have wild parties and cook-outs. I don't know what it is, but those people are not right."

At that moment, Moms and I looked at each other and cracked a smile. Moms handled the situation with grace, as she always did. "Thanks for the great welcome to the neighborhood. I'm sure we'll be great friends pretty soon. Thanks for dropping by."

I lifted my hot lips from the pie, and mumbled, "Thank you Mr. and Mrs. Robinson, I will be over soon. Leave the windows open so I can smell that good food." We all laughed, and Mrs. Robinson said, "You two are always welcome. We are going back home, welcome to Charlotte. Bye babies." Mr. Robinson shook me and Moms' hand firmly, then they went back home.

As soon as the Robinsons left, Moms and I shook hands, and busted out laughing. I said, "Mr. Robinson doesn't know it, but he just described our whole neighborhood in Harlem, including us!"

Moms replied, "Yeah Son, he sure did. I like the family feel down here. I think this will be great for us."

"You know how we do Moms; this radio is coming on right now. Out of respect for the Robinsons, let's take it easy for now." I played Mary J's version of the classic song *Sweet Thing*.

"I like your style Son, now let's finish unpacking." This had been a long day, so Moms and I called it an early night. Moms had a meeting at her new job the next day and she wanted to be well rested to make a great first impression. She won't admit it but I think that she picked up that idea from my Pops.

The next morning I woke up home alone in a big house in Charlotte, North Carolina. If I was in Harlem, this would've been the perfect place for the House Party of the Year. I looked at my phone, and I had two missed calls from Tone, and a text message from Maria, making sure I got here safely. I was so tired, that I forgot to call Tone last night, so I hit him up.

"Country Boy, what's good? You start milking cows and forget about the little people?"

"You are a funny guy Block Head. We were tired last night, but you will be pleased to know that the house is crazy! You will have your own room when you come down to visit."

"What's up with the country gals out there? What are they looking like?" I told him to chill out, because I hadn't been outside yet. At the same moment, I heard some music blasting. It was *Rolling in the Deep*, by Adele, a song that I liked and we listened to back home. I said, "Block Head, let me call you back in a little while. Don't break any helmets before I do."

He laughed. "Cool, don't get you chair stuck in the dirt, while farming crops out there."

I went outside to see where that loud music was coming from, and of course it was the Kelly household. This is what the Robinsons told us about last night. I thought to myself, "If you have good taste in music, then you can't be that bad." Besides, I wasn't doing anything else so I rolled over to the Kelly house. I noticed when we moved in that they also had a ramp in front of their house.

The Kelly's Residence was a two story home with a long driveway that led to a garage. There was a basketball hoop placed over the front of the garage, and a motorcycle was parked in the front. The grass was neatly cut, and there was a big peace sign on the front door. I didn't know what to expect, but I knew meeting the new neighbors would be better than sitting at home all day. As I got closer, the music got even louder. That Adele song must have been on repeat, because it started over again. I rolled up the ramp and rang the bell. After about two minutes I rang the bell again, but there was no answer. I waited until the song was about to start over to ring it one more time. No one asked who was at the door, but I could hear them opening it. I didn't hear any lock turn, so this let me know that the door was unlocked. I quickly thought to myself, "In Harlem, two things that we make sure to do are always lock our doors, and definitely ask who it is before opening the door. You may never know who is on the other side of that door."

When the door opened, there stood an average height, skinny white boy with a fire red Mohawk, freckles, a Boston Celtics jersey and basketball shorts on. I figured that he was maybe 13 or 14 years old, due to the red peach fuzz growing on his face.

"What's up, can I help you?"

"What's good man? My name is Party Artie from Harlem, New York and my mother and I just moved into the house next door. What's up with that Celtics jersey? Are you from Boston?"

Ryan shook his head, "No, my parents and relatives are from Ireland, so I roll with team that has the Leprechaun and the luck of the Irish. My name is Ryan, man, welcome to the neighborhood. "

I laughed. "Ok, thanks, man. That was close, because New Yorkers don't like any teams from Boston, and Boston fans are crazy. I was surprised that you guys have a ramp. Does everyone out here have ramps in front of their houses?"

Ryan answered "No, not really, but our grandmother comes to visit us a lot. She has a wheelchair, but it's not as cool as yours is."

"Thanks, everyone can't ride in style like I do." As we gave each other a hand shake and started laughing, the music stopped, and I heard a voice coming from inside the house.

"Ryan why do you have the door open, you are letting the cold air out and the flies in." Within seconds that voice had a face attached to it. She was tall, athletic, with a red pony tail, freckles, and some pretty green eyes. She was wearing some blue jean shorts, with a T-shirt that said *Wild Girls Have More Fun*. She also had some pretty toes that were painted with navy blue polish. She definitely would have been considered a winner back home. She saw me, and said, "Oh, I didn't see you, can we help you?"

"Hello, I am your new neighbor, Arthur, from New York City, nice to meet you. Maybe you can show me around the neighborhood later, while we get some ice cream."

She folded her arms. "I don't think so, but welcome to the neighborhood. You are letting the cold air out, so you are either in or out of the house." Just like that she went back upstairs and turned her radio back on. I didn't want Ryan to feel funny, so I smiled and said, "It's all good, man, she is no joke."

"That's my older sister Jennifer," he replied. "She is grouchy all of the time. Don't worry about it. Arthur, I thought that you said your name was Party Artie."

"Listen young man, when dealing with the ladies, you have to be smooth. Good thing I moved here when I did, so you can learn from the master." He laughed again and said, "I knew how to get turned down way before you moved here." We both laughed, and gave each other a five. Ryan picked up his cell phone and called a number. He said, "Mom, I just met the new neighbor, and he is very cool. Can we have him and his mom over for dinner tonight?" He listened for a moment. "Okay, thanks Mom, goodbye." He turned back to me. "My mom said you guys should come over tonight around 7 o'clock for dinner."

"That sounds cool, thanks. We'll see you later. I still have some unpacking to do."

I sent Moms a text message, to let her know that I had met half of the Kelly family, and that we were invited to dinner.

Moms got home at about 6pm that day. I heard the truck pulling in to the driveway, so I greeted her at the door. "Hello pretty lady, how was your first day at the office?" She kissed me on my forehead. "Hey Prince, it was okay. We just had meetings and workshops all day. Let me take a shower and change my clothes for tonight. Were the Kelly family as wild and crazy as we heard?" I laughed and said "No, they were cool. I just met the kids, and they seemed pretty normal to me."

When Moms was ready, we walked over to the Kelly home. There was a Red 2010 Honda Civic parked in the driveway. Moms rang the bell, tapped my arm, and said "Listen to that Son, someone in there is playing *Let's Get It On*. I like the Kelly family already." *Let's Get It On* was Moms' favorite song, performed by the late great Marvin Gaye. I smiled and nodded at Moms, and then the door quickly opened. "Welcome to Charlotte neighbors! I'm Christina Kelly, but please call me Chris. Make yourself at home." It was Ryan's Mom, and she was definitely fine as ever. She looked like she could be Jennifer's older sister but with brown hair, instead of red. Moms quickly responded, "How are you doing? I'm Paula Thomas, and this is my Prince Arthur. I love your choice in music girl. What do you know about Marvin? That was my boyfriend back in the days. He just didn't know about it." They shook hands and laughed, while I shook my head.

"Nice to meet you Mrs. Kelly, I see where Jennifer gets her looks, and good taste in music," I said.

Mrs. Kelly laughed. "Thank you, young man, why don't you two come on in, and get comfortable. Dinner is almost ready. Mr. Kelly is closing a sale at the dealership, so he'll join us a little later. I prepared a traditional Irish meal to welcome you guys into the neighborhood. I haven't made something like this in a while."

She directed us to the bathroom to wash our hands, and straight to the dinner table. She wanted us to enjoy this meal in the worst way. A few minutes after we came in, my man Ryan came downstairs eating a chocolate bar. "My main man Artie, what's up man? Glad you came over. Nice to meet you Ma'am, my name is Ryan."

Mrs. Kelly said, "Ryan, throw that junk away. We are about to sit down for a real meal."

"Okay Mom, but let's not forget about the wicked witch upstairs. I'll go get her." He went back upstairs, and then returned with Jennifer. She was cooler than I expected.

"Hello Ma'am, nice to meet you, my name is Jennifer. Welcome to Charlotte. Hello Arthur, good to see you again."

"Nice to meet you as well, you are a pretty little thing aren't you?" Moms said. Ryan quickly replied, "No offense, Mrs. Thomas, but you must have left your glasses in your suitcase." Everybody laughed at that one, even Jennifer.

Mrs. Kelly brought out dish after dish. What a meal! She started off with potato soup, and it was pretty good. Ten minutes later, she said, "We usually eat this for Sunday breakfast, but since you are special guests, I made some farl." I had to say something at this point. "Mrs. Kelly, we appreciate the great music, and the hospitality, and the potato soup was banging, but I think we may have to pass on the farl!" Everyone exploded into laughter, and Ryan got up and shook my hand.

Jennifer said, "Don't worry Arthur, farl is homemade potato bread, and it's very good."

"I trust you, cutie, so I will try it."

She shook her head. "Whatever." She was right, it was very good. Mrs. Kelly made something called spiced beef, cabbage, and potato champ, which was really mashed potatoes, and she topped it off with some Irish Apple Pie. We laughed and talked while eating this tasty dinner. "Mrs. K, that was a great meal, but you have me feeling like Mr. Potato Head right now! I might gain 20 pounds if I eat over here all of the time," I said.

Moms said, "Be quiet boy, you are a mess." Everyone laughed. Mrs. Kelly said, "We love to treat our company like family, but we will take it easy on you next time."

"Arthur let's go into the den and play some video games, and Jen why don't you show him your picture album, so he can see some of your friends. Maybe he'll leave you alone, when he sees how a real girl looks," Ryan suggested.

She said, "Shut up little guy. Let's go Arthur."

Mrs. K agreed. "That's a great idea, now Paula and I can talk over a cup of coffee."

The den was full of pictures and trophies. I was impressed by the plaques that were on the wall, and the trophies that were everywhere. I saw men's basketball, baseball trophies and also women's softball, tennis, and track trophies. I said, "Wow, your parents really did their thing. That's a lot of winning that they did."

Jennifer put her hands on her hips, and rolled her eyes, "Excuse me, ten of those trophies belong to me. I'm not all looks and brains." I could barely begin to start my line about beauty and being an athlete when the door bell rang. Jennifer said, "That's my boyfriend, see you guys later." Just like that, she was gone. I didn't even get a chance to see the guy, because she flew out of the door. I was starting to get tired, because it had been a long day for me. I played one more game of Madden with Ryan, and then I told him that I would holler at him tomorrow.

I went in to the kitchen to see if Moms was ready, and I overheard her and Mrs. K talking. Moms said, "We have two schools in mind for Arthur, Franklin Tech, and Parkville High School. They both are in the area, plus they have ramps, and provide transportation for wheel chair students."

"Parkville High is where he needs to go. It is a fine school, and we are very pleased with the way that they treat special needs students," Mrs. K answered. Moms looked at Mrs. K and said "What do you mean, Chris? How do you know about that?"

"Jennifer was diagnosed with Attention Deficit Disorder in the 5th grade by a school psychologist. The school suggested that we get her tested since she was displaying a quick temper, and was losing focus and not paying attention while in class. Jennifer is taking classes with fewer students, which are centered on helping her focus better. The teachers are compassionate and sensitive to every child's needs at Parkville. Besides, Arthur will already have a friend and a neighbor that goes there. They are both in the 12th grade, so they will be around to support each other."

Moms said, "Chris, I usually don't listen to salesman on the first try, but you make a good case for Parkville. I'll definitely look into it. Girl, when we get settled in, you're definitely welcomed for dinner. It may not be this many potatoes, but I can throw down in the kitchen as well." They hugged each other and started laughing. I interrupted.

"Now I really feel like the Prince, with two beautiful women in my presence, with those beautiful smiles. Are you ready to go my Queen?"

"Yes, son, it is time to go." Mrs. K loved my sweet talk. "Arthur you are the cutest little thing, thank you for paying us a visit tonight." As we were leaving, a Navy Blue 2009 Ford Ram was pulling up into the driveway. Mr. Kelly got out of the truck and he stood about 6 feet tall. He had on a suit and his belly stuck out from his shirt. You could tell that he was an athlete back in the day, because of his broad shoulders and his muscular frame. He shook me and Moms' hands and said "Good evening, I'm Daniel Kelly, but please call me Dan. I'm sorry I missed dinner, but I had a sale to close at the car dealership. When Mrs. Kelly has new visitors, she always cooks a feast. I know that my wife was excited tonight, so there will be plenty of potatoes left for me eat." When he said that, we all busted out laughing. Moms said, "Good evening, I'm Paula Thomas, and this is my son Arthur. I think that there are a few left for you, sir. You have a beautiful family. Thank you for the hospitality. Good night, we will speak soon." I said, "Good night Mr. K, I heard you were a Celtics fan, and we are a strictly a Knicks family, so we have some work to do." He shook my hand, and said "I guess we do young man, good night to you two. Welcome to Charlotte."

Chapter Four- Parkville High

Everyone is finally seated, and Natalie Perry just finished singing Mariah Carey's classic song *Hero*. I see people clapping, hear some cheering, and even see a few crying. She definitely did her thing with that song. Ms. Palmore just grabbed the microphone, "Good morning to all of the family who've come from near and far, friends, and especially to the Graduating class of Parkville High School! This is a special class we have this year, folks. This group of students has displayed intellect, determination, talent, style, and more importantly class. I am honored to announce the graduating class of 2012!" The crowd just erupted and applauded Ms. Palmore, and my fellow graduates. I am sitting thinking about my first day at Parkville when I met Ms. P.

I woke up on Monday morning at 6:00am, and I was excited and anxious about my first day at Parkville High. I looked in my closet for something fresh to throw on for my debut at my new school. I found a yellow polo shirt with the light blue logo that I could wear with my yellow Yankee fitted cap. My shirt was a little wrinkled, so I ironed it to make sure that it looked crisp and sharp. I had on some light blue jeans and some white and yellow Nike Air Force Ones. I threw on my yellow canary diamond ear rings to match. I also sprayed a little of my Sean John cologne behind each ear and on my neck and wrists. Had to look and smell good, as my Dad always told me.

I went to the kitchen after I was satisfied with my outfit. There was a note on the table, along with some toast, bacon, and eggs. *Have a great first day Prince, Love Mom.* Beep, Beep, Beep, I heard a loud horn outside the house. It was the Special Transportation Service, which provided a ride back and forth to school for me. They were just like the Access-A-Ride we had back in Harlem. When I got on the shuttle, I met Ralph, the bus driver. He was a slim white dude with a low haircut, and a sharp goatee. He was a lot younger and cooler than I thought he would be. He said, "What's up my man? Are you trying to be late for your first day, and ruin my reputation? I'm Ralph, and you're lucky because you're the only one on my route at your school."

"Good morning man, I'm Arthur. That's cool; I always knew that the Prince would have his own personal driver one day." We both laughed and shook hands.

The school was about 30 minutes from the house, but it was a cool ride, because I got a chance to see what stores were in town. Ralph was cool though, and he loved music. He played everything from Jay Z and Kanye West to Cold Play and Pearl Jam. When we finally got there, Ralph looked back and said, "Last stop kid, see you at 3 o'clock."

I took a deep breath, and said to myself, "Let's go Party Artie, its show time. You're from Harlem so you can make it anywhere." The school was huge, and I saw ramps on both sides, so I would be able to get around with no problem. Right away I saw a few cuties walking into the school. "Good morning sweetheart, enjoy your day. You look nice today." I must have used those lines at least 5 times before I even got into the school. The kids were friendly, and they were not dressed as badly as I thought that they would be.

There were definitely a few fashion don'ts that I witnessed. There were a few girls with open toe shoes with stockings on, and some dudes with their shirts tucked in, and buttoned tightly up to the top. I did see a few gold teeth as well, but they were cool for the most part. As soon as I went into the school, there she was, Ms. Palmore.

"Stop running Michael, and Tasha watch your mouth young lady!" she screamed out. She was dark brown with shoulder length hair, and she was tall. She had on a tan skirt with a matching top, with some heels my mother would love. She was definitely attractive, and I hoped that I was in her class no matter what it was. She looked at me with her dark brown eyes, and said "Good morning, I'm Ms. Palmore, the principal here at Parkville High. Welcome to the school. What part of New York are you from?"

I paused for a second, as I got myself together and said, "Good morning, my name is Arthur Thomas, and my mother and I just moved here from Harlem. Congratulations on being the principal, that's a real power move. You look very nice today, and those shoes are the truth if you don't mind me saying so. How did you know that I am from New York?"

She laughed. "Thanks for the kind words. I have been down here long enough to know when a New Yorker comes into town. I'm from Long Island, but I stayed down here after college. Welcome to our school, you will like it here. There is the main office to your left. Give them your name, and you can get your class schedule. Good luck to you, Arthur."

While I was in the office getting my schedule, I saw a poster on the wall and a flyer on the desk. It was an announcement that Parkville High would be participating in the town's annual Special Olympics on the following Saturday. All participants who were eligible should register by Wednesday. I figured that this would be a chance for me to meet some people, and to impress some of the local young ladies with my athletic skills. I felt little funny about the Special Olympics though. I didn't want people to think that I was a charity case. People in the past have felt sorry for me, and treated me with extra care since I was in a wheelchair. Until they got to know me better of course, and found out that I can handle myself just fine.

The first day was cool; classes are just as boring in Charlotte as they were in Harlem. Some things don't change. One good thing was that Jennifer was in my English class, so I already had a friend. When I got home, I told Moms about my first day of school, and then I mentioned the Olympics, which had been on my mind all day, besides the thought of taking Ms. P to the movies one day. I talked it over with my Moms.

"Moms, there is a Special Olympics coming up, but I don't think I'm with it. I don't want people to feel sorry for me or think that I'm different. I'm way too cool for that."

"Prince, I think you should go for it. This will be a chance to meet new friends and to show off the skills that your father passed down to you. Let me tell you something, Son. Don't ever think you are too cool to try a new experience. You'll only be putting limits on yourself. You'll also be depriving the world of a chance to see the Young Prince in action! Son, when you give your best effort in a situation, you cannot lose."

I thought about it, and as usual Moms was right. That's why there is only one Queen. "I'll go for it," I told her. To celebrate, we shared a dance to Melissa Morgan's *Fool's Paradise*, and then we filled out the forms.

The week went by pretty quickly; I got a few phone numbers from the young ladies at school and got a lot of compliments on my fresh outfits. My mind was set on the Special Olympics, though. I guess word travels fast everywhere, because people were approaching me in the halls, in class, and in the lunch room. "Hey New York, I heard that you signed up for the Olympics. I can't wait to see you in action." I heard that from both girls and the guys. I didn't know if they truly wanted me to win, or if they wanted to see Party Artie from the big city lose to the country boys. I kept my swagger at all times, because Pops taught me to never let them see me sweat. "No doubt, I will be in the winner's circle representing Harlem and of course Parkville High. Charge your cell phones, so that you can take pictures!"

On my first Wednesday, during my last period math class, Ms. P walked in looking as fine as ever. My math teacher stopped in his tracks and said, "Students, settle down and give Ms. Palmore your full attention." Ms. P had a look that was no joke. She was normally very cool, but if she was serious, then you would automatically straighten up. I saw her in action that Tuesday when she caught two boys smoking in the bathroom. Ms, P sent them home right away, and dished out one week suspensions for both of them.

"Sorry to interrupt the class Mr. Irvin, but I need to see Arthur Thomas right away." A few people looked concerned for me, but then I heard a voice from the middle of the classroom, "Uh oh, Wheels of Steel, you're in trouble. You must've been double parked by the cafeteria." About half of the class laughed, and a few people giggled.

"Steven, that is not cool. Knock it off!" Ms. P yelled.

This is was the first time I noticed Steven Ross. He was a cool looking white dude. He was very tall, definitely over 6 feet with dirty blond hair. He was muscular, and he must have played some kind of sport, because he had on Parkville High Shorts and T-shirt, with some Nike slippers on. I played it cool, and said, "Don't worry about me classmates; I am always good, and I know all of the parking rules around here. Steve, good one, you are a funny dude."

As I was leaving the classroom, a girl that was sitting right next to me tapped me on my arm. I remembered her name was Stacy, when Mr. Irvin read the attendance sheet earlier. She hasn't said a word in class all week; she was brown skinned, with two straightened afro puffs that she wore in her hair. She was a little on the chubby side, but she was still a cutie. She whispered, "Don't worry about Steven, he is a jerk." I winked at her as I was leaving the class room. When we got outside, Ms. P said, "Sorry about that Arthur, not everyone is polite at Parkville High."

"That's nothing Ms. P, I'm from Harlem, and trust me, when it comes to the wheelchair jokes, I've heard them all!" We both laughed, and then she said, "You need to meet with your coach and your teammates for the Special Olympics next Saturday. Your Shuttle bus will pick you up at 4pm to take you home today, instead of 3 o'clock today."

"Cool, Ms. P, can I keep my first place trophy in your office, so that I can visit it everyday?"

"Arthur, don't be inappropriate with me! Get back to class! Good luck with the Olympics, and make us proud." Ms. P was something else, because she could make you feel like you were the man and a chump in one conversation.

Chapter Five- Special Olympics

After math class was over, I went to the gym to meet my teammates and coach. There was only one person in the gym, Coach Woods. He was about 6 feet tall with a serious beer belly. He looked like he could be related to my neighbor Mr. Robinson. He even had the same old school George Jefferson haircut with the afro on the side and he was bald in the middle.

As I rolled over to him I thought, "What has Moms gotten me into this time?" I shook his hand and said "What's good coach; I'm Arthur Thomas, your go-to player. What's the game plan? Am I the only one on the team?" He said" I'm Coach Woods Son, and you are right; we are going to be champions. There are only two of you, and Hector should be here in a minute."

I asked him, "Is he in a wheelchair too?"

Coach Woods said, "No, Hector is what the experts call 'mentally challenged,' which means he has an intellectual disability. As a matter of fact, there's Hector right there so you can see for yourself."

I turned around and looked across the gym, and saw a smooth Puerto Rican dude walking across the gym. I was shocked to see a Puerto Rican down here in Charlotte.

"Wait for me coach; the Boricua Boy is here to bring home the gold!" Hector was about 6 feet 1, athletic and has this dark brown curly hair. He had on a lime green sweat suit, with some lime green and white Nike sneakers. I did notice that he had some cherry red lip stick on his cheek. I thought to myself "He needs some work, but he is not a lost cause." He reminded me of my man Pablo from back home. Pablo was always fresh and smooth with the ladies.

Hector was definitely not shy. He shook my hand and gave me a man hug, and then said, "What's up man, nice to meet you. That is a sharp chair that you are sporting. My name is Hector, and I like your style already, teammate. Do you think that you can hook up my shoe laces like that?" I always had them laced uptown style, skipping holes to make them bounce right.

"Thanks a lot," I said. "My name is Party Artie, and I can show you how to hook up your kicks, but the first lesson is going to be to have them on the right foot."

Hector looked down, and I laughed and said, "Just messing with you, sure, I will teach you."

He said, "Oh, you got jokes. Thanks, man." We shook hands and laughed. We didn't really practice, but we did tell coach what event that we would be participating in. Coach told us that since we only had two people participating, that we could only choose one event. Hector signed up for the 100 meter race.

I said, "You must be a speedster, because you signed up for the fastest race."

"I have to be fast to keep up with all of my ladies."

"No doubt Hector, I feel you. Coach, I am signing up for the 300 meter wheelchair race."

Hector said, "What's up with the slow poke race, Arthur?"

I told him, "Young Man, one day you will learn that it is better to last longer than to be the fastest."

Coach Woods chimed in and said, "I hope that you boys are still talking about track and field." Hector and I both laughed and shook hands. While Coach was in his office filling out paperwork, Hector and I got to talk a little bit more. I said, "I have been here all week, and this is this first time I've seen you. Are all of your classes upstairs?" Hector responded, "No, I was supposed to graduate last year, but I fell one class short. So I only take an English class on Wednesday and Friday. I just got hired at Mr. Green's grocery store a few miles away. Working will give me a chance to make money, and stay away from my house."

I said "Oh, okay there's nothing wrong with being a Super Senior and making some money. Now I know how you got that lip stick on your cheek. Why don't you like being in the crib? Is your Moms always on your case?"

"I wish I had a nagging mother. I live in the group home on Eager Street, and I don't remember my parents. They gave me away to the state when I was two years old. When I have kids and a wife, I will never let them go."

I was shocked to be having such a serious conversation with my new friend. "I'm sorry to hear that man, but you are definitely hanging in there. They would be proud of who you are today." Hector shook my hand, looked at the clock and said, "Thanks Bro, excuse me for a second."

He ran over to the water fountain, and pulled out two pills from his pocket. He waited when the clock hit exactly 4pm, then he took the pills. He came back like nothing happened.

I said "Look Hector, I want to win these Olympics too, but I don't think we need you to be juicing to get it done. Just say no to drugs, kid."

Hector laughed. "Na, Bro this is my medication, I have to take it at 7am, 4pm, and 9pm before bed. It helps to control my mood, and keep me calm throughout the day.

"Okay kid, whatever it takes I guess, let me get your number before I jet. My chariot is outside." We exchanged numbers, and then I went outside as Ralph was pulling up with the shuttle.

"What's up Ralph? What do you know about the group home on Eager Street?" Ralph looked at me from his rear view mirror, and said, "That is what they call the Crazy House. Everyone that lives there has issues. Those people are retarded, and should be kept in isolation."

"Come on Ralph, that's not even cool to say." He pulled over and sat next to me, and then he said, "You didn't hear me out Artie, that is what *they* say. Who I am talking about are the ones that have never been exposed to anyone that may be going through different situations in life. Thanks to this job, I have had the privilege to go the movies, to basketball games, and to dinner with the mentally challenged individuals that I serve. I know first hand that we are all the same. One time while we were out I turned around to look at a pretty woman, and sure enough, one of my clients was looking too. He shook my hand, and said, "I know that you saw that too Ralph."

Ralph and I both laughed. "No doubt Ralph, I would be the last to judge a book by its cover. Thanks for the talk. You are a good dude Ralph."

After dinner that night, I called my man Tone back home.

"What's going on Country Boy, how are things out there?" Tone asked me.

"So far so good Brother, I can't complain about too much. The ladies are definitely fine down here, and they are much friendlier than in Harlem."

Tone chimed in, "Don't forget to hook me up when I come down there. Make sure you send their pictures to my phone in advance though. No room for mistakes on that one. How is the new school?"

"I like it so far Tone, it is a very big school, and most of the kids are cool. The Principal is a beautiful sister from Long Island. Oh yeah, that reminds me, I signed up for the Special Olympics next week, and I need you to go to the t-shirt spot on 125th Street. I need a fresh uniform for next Saturday. I'll send you the money tomorrow. Get a pen, so I can tell you exactly what I want on it."

Tone said, "I got your back kid, but these double football practices have me beat. Text me the information, and I'll take care of it for you tomorrow. I'll holler at you later." The following Thursday, when I got home from school, there was a box in front of the house. My boy Tone had come through for me, as I expected. I held the box on my lap with my left hand, while I controlled the wheel with my right hand. When I opened the box, it instantly reminded me of Harlem. Two things that we loved to do back home were pop tags on new clothes and wear brand new sneakers. Tone sent me a royal blue and gray sweat suit (our school colors) some fresh White Nike Air Force Ones, a new white Nike head band, and course my t-shirt. It said *Parkville* on the front (which was the original uniform), but on the back it had a number six to represent my favorite Ball player Lebron King James. But it also had my nickname on it, Party Artie. Now I was definitely ready for Saturday's event. I texted Tone to thank him, he responded by texting "No doubt Bro, make us proud.

HARLEM Stand Up!"

Finally Saturday morning was here, and I was ready except for one thing. I went to my bathroom, and pulled out my clippers. I gave myself a haircut and a shape up to make sure I was completely fresh. Even though I was going to a race, I still sprayed a little of my Sean John smell goods on. I had to be prepared to meet my future wife there. My shuttle bus came to the house at 7am to pick me up, because the athletes needed to be there a little earlier than the crowd. I only ate a piece of toast and drank some juice, because I wanted to stay light in my chair. Moms kissed me on my forehead, and said, "Looking good Prince, good luck today. The Kelly family and I will be there to see you in action. Love you."

"Thanks Moms, make some room for the medal or trophy that I will be winning today. Make sure that you point out to Jennifer how fresh I look today. Love you too, see you later."

On time as usual, I heard Ralph honk the horn, and I was out. Ralph said, "I am usually off on Saturdays, but I had to support my main man, Party Artie! Besides, I am getting paid overtime, and there will be some fine women in the crowd today. I'm proud of you kid, good luck today."

I said, "Good looking Ralph, I will do my thing today. These folks have never seen anything like me before."

The event was held at the track of the University of North Carolina at Charlotte, so the ride was a little longer than usual. From the moment I got there, I could feel the excitement. People were outside of the track with barbecue grills, and signs and flags of the schools that they represented. I wasn't aware of how many people support and participate in the Special Olympics. There was music, pretty girls, and cameras, all before 8am in the morning.

In Harlem, people love to be in the spotlight, and the center of attention, but we don't usually come out this early. It was cool though, that meant that there would be more people for me to impress with my style and my skills. When Ralph and I got to the front of the track, Hector and Coach Woods greeted us at the gate. Hector had on some short royal blue shorts, a gray Parkville High tank top, with some white Puma track shoes on. "Looking good Artie, but what about me, don't I look like a champion?"

I said, "You are looking like Usain Bolt today, Rico Suave, like you are about to win every race. I see you are showing a little thigh for the ladies."

We all laughed at that one, even Coach Woods.

"Prince, there goes my baby!" Of course it was Moms, along with the Kelly family. My little man Ryan came up to me, and said, "What's up Arthur, I know you will do well today. You are looking very sharp today. Only thing that you are missing is some Celtic green for good luck."

I said, "It's all good Lil Bro, I will be just fine. I might not break a sweat today. Good morning Mr. and Mrs. K, thanks for coming out to support me."

Mrs. K said, "We wouldn't have missed it for the world Arthur, now do your best today." My classmate Jennifer was there. She said, "Good luck today Arthur, you look very nice today. Doesn't he look sharp today Steven?" As soon as I heard that, I looked next to Jennifer, and there he was, Steven Ross, the funny guy from my math class. He still had on his Parkville High Basketball T shirt and shorts with those same Nike slippers. He said, "Yes, Sweetie, he looks good. Let me show him where the track is."

Then he escorted me over to where Coach and Hector were standing. "Good luck to you, Wheels of Steel!" Then he looked over at my teammate, and said, "Good luck to you Hector Loco! Just remember to stay off of the grass. The race is on the track."

I laughed and said, "Good looking Steve, remember that it's ok to wear some regular clothes every once in a while." Hector must have missed the comment, because he said, "Thanks Steven, see you later." As soon as I began to explain to Hector how much of a jerk Steven was, I heard something else loud and clear.

The master of ceremonies voice blasted over the loud speaker, "Will the participants for the 300 meter wheelchair race report to the track!" He announced Frank Jones from Parsons High School and Mike Hansen from Franklin Tech. When it was time to announce me, he said "The next athlete is from Parkville High School and he is a newcomer to the Olympics. So give a warm welcome to Arthur Thomas."

People gave me a pretty nice applause. I heard a few people commenting on my outfit. "I hope he races as well as he looks. That kid is a sharp dresser." I heard someone say," He must have a hot date later on." I laughed to myself, because I love when people notice and admire my stylish ways. I went over to the other athletes and said hello and good luck. They looked at each other and shook their heads. They knew that they would be in for a tough race. Before I knew what happened, there was a big roar for Randy Stokes. Parents, fellow athletes, the cheerleaders, and even the judges stood up and clapped for this guy. Frank told me that he was the defending champ for all of the wheelchair events. When I looked at Randy, he was cool too. He was about 5 feet 7, brown skin, with a short hair cut. He had on a fresh black Champion sweat suit with a gold C on the chest, with some brand new gold and black Nike Air Max sneakers on. He would have given me some competition, but his shoe laces were all wrong. He had them choked up to the top, with every hole laced. I know that his feet couldn't breathe in those things.

Randy rolled over to me to shake hands and said, "What's good man? I'm Randy Stokes from Philly. I guess you didn't think you would meet somebody like you out here huh? I moved to Raleigh with my folks about two years ago."

I said, "Yeah man, I see you are doing your thing out here, you have Superstar Status." I shook his hand, and said, "My name is Party Artie from Harlem, New York, I don't want to take all of your shine, but I need some of it. I hope there is room at the top." We both laughed, Randy said, "It's all good my man, there's always room. Good luck with the race. I won't be too hard on you."

"No doubt kid, good luck."

When the race started, I felt confident even though Randy got off to a fast start. After the first 100 meters, we were separated from the other two racers. After the first turn on the track, I felt tired and my arms were getting weak. Randy had built a three stride lead on me. I had not been outside much since we had moved here, so I was a little bit out of shape. I knew one thing for sure, is that I cannot come down here and lose my first race in front of all these people. I would be finished before I even got started. I didn't plan on breaking much of a sweat today, but Randy brought the best out of me. My head band was originally there for style, but it kept the sweat from pouring into my eyes. I turned it up to my next level. My arms were on fire, but I was gaining ground on him with 50 meters to go.

The crowd was jumping up and down and cheering loudly. This reminded me of being on the block in Harlem. I was right behind Randy at this point, and I knew that I could catch him, but I was running out of time. The finish line was 20 meters away, and I was right next to Randy. I could feel the breeze coming from Randy and his chair. I gave it one last burst of power, and then I finally broke away from Randy just in time to cross the finish line. We couldn't even hear each other say good race, because the roar from the crowd was deafening.

The master of ceremonies picked up the microphone, and said, "Please folks, another round of applause for all four racers, this was the best wheelchair race that we have ever seen at these Olympics! Please folks give it up for our defending champ Randy, and our new Champ Party Artie (he must have read my shirt) Great race guys."

"Good race Randy. You have many skills with that chair. Let's keep in touch." Randy said, "Yeah man that was a good one. Congrats on the victory. I am in about four more events so my medal count will be minus one, but it's cool because I lost to a true champion. I'll get your phone number before we leave."

As I was leaving the track, I saw Stacy sitting on the bleachers with her head buried in a book. I said, "Good morning, friend. I know that you didn't come out here so early to do some extra reading."

She said, "Good job, with the race, but you almost lost because you were being cocky." Then she stuck her head back into her book. I said "For someone who is so shy, you always have something strong to say. You are right; I almost blew it, thinking that I was the only one with skills. I'll see you in class on Monday, and you better talk to me." She laughed and said "Okay, congratulations again, Parkville in the house!"

Chapter Six –Rico Suave

"Hector Alvarez!" Ms. P yelled out, and of course the crowd cheered and yelled as she called my partner in crime, Hector Alvarez, a.k.a. Rico Suave. I call him Rico Suave, because he thinks he's the ultimate ladies man. He thinks every girl either loves him or hates him because they can't have him. I must admit, some of the chicks like Hector, and he definitely loves all of them. I almost forgot, Hector won his Special Olympics race, and he actually set a record at the event. I really feel proud to see Hector walk across that stage; minus the Miami Vice look he is sporting. "No Hector, not the sunglasses, white suit, pink T-shirt and white shoes without any socks!"

Everyone always judges Hector because he is mentally challenged, but he is just fine to me. Hector does show some signs of his disability, when he has to make a quick decision or do any critical thinking. But his spirit and work ethic always helps him overcome the situation. I remember when Hector first got his job at Mr. Green's grocery store.

When Hector first got the job, Steven came by to give him a rough time. "Hector Loco, where is the bread, where is the juice, where are the light bulbs?" When Steven saw no one was amused by his antics, Hector told me Steven finally left the store and never came back. Hector mainly does stock in the store, but he also does the deliveries to nearby customers. When Hector does deliveries, the customers must have exact change, because it takes Hector a little longer to do the calculations. All his customers enjoy Hector's service because he's always laughing and in a good mood. He takes pride in getting people their groceries in a timely manner. He has this saying he uses with all his customers: "Since you're my favorite customer, I hope you enjoyed my service as much as I enjoyed serving you." With lines like that, he always gets a good tip. One time Hector's hard work ethic almost got him in trouble. A food delivery came in, but Mr. Green wasn't at the store yet. Hector wanted to show Mr. Green how hard he'd worked. Instead of putting the food away according to which

———

food group they belonged to, he put them away in alphabetical order. Hector felt terrible about his mistake. "Mr. Green, am I going to get fired for this?" Mr. Green said, "No Hector its okay. It was a good idea, but that's not how things run here. To be honest I don't think my customers know their alphabets as well as you do. It would only confuse them."

I'm very proud of Rico Suave. Despite his challenges, he got his diploma, and received a full scholarship to the local technical college. He helped me convince Moms to let me take driving lessons. Coming from the city I was used to taking public transportation, but Hector told me, that in order to take the girls out in this town, I had to have access to a car. He taught me the importance of saving money. He bought his car by saving his tips from work and some of the money that he gets from the State. Hector is a great friend.

Chapter Seven -Jay Lo

"Jennifer Kelly!"

Wow, we are halfway through graduation. Ms. P just called my home girl and neighbor, Jay Lo. Students, teachers, and parents cheered and clapped loudly for her. Jay Lo is very popular in the school. She became the star of the women's soccer team, during this year. Jennifer is a sweetheart, but she is not the one to get upset. I remember early this school year Jay Lo had problems with our English teacher Mr. Donahue. Jay became very frustrated one day, when he kept asking her the same question, so she knocked all of her books off her desk. She was quickly sent to the Principals' office. That was the day that Ms. P suggested that she tries out for the school soccer team as a way to channel her aggression and to improve her focus. Since she was a natural athlete, she could play any sport. Of course this was a natural fit for Jay Lo. She quickly became the star of the team.

Jennifer and I got really cool throughout the school year. I think all of those nights of studying for Mr. Donahue's tests really helped our friendship. We also used to read our papers and projects to each other, to get an honest opinion.

Jay Lo is definitely a loyal friend who has my back. I remember late in November, Jay Lo stopped me in the hallway, and said, "Hey Arthur, what are you and Mrs. Thomas doing for Thanksgiving? Are you going to New York?" I said "Hey cutie, I'm not sure yet. All of our family is either in New York or Chicago. My Moms has to work that Friday, so I think we will be staying in Charlotte this year." She said "Let us know, because we would love for you two to join us at our house for dinner." I smiled and said "Thanks for the offer; I think Moms and I would enjoy that. I'll talk to her tonight. She'll call your mom later."

Moms and I gladly accepted the offer for Thanksgiving dinner. Moms cooked some oxtails, ribs, macaroni and cheese, and potato salad to bring over. The night was filled with laughter, good music, and food. Jay Lo was on my team in charades, and we lost all of the games, because she wasn't paying attention to my clues. But it was all good, because we all had a ball that night.

We went to all of Jennifer's games, and she was faster and stronger than all of the other girls. Even though there were a lot of cuties on the soccer team, her red ponytail was always a show-stopper. She used to say, "Arthur, I hope the only reason that you come to my games is not to look at my teammates."

"Of course not Jay Lo, you are my favorite player. I just come to make sure that you have a stylish cheering section."

Jennifer led Parkville High all the way to the County Championship game, which they lost 2 to 1 in a thriller. Jay Lo turned out to be the MVP of our Team, and is receiving a full scholarship to play soccer at the University of North Carolina at Charlotte. All of her teammates are still standing up for her and Steven just gave her a dozen roses. "There you go Steve; you finally made a smooth move!" I yelled out.

Chapter Eight- Spring Break

Ms. P was still at the microphone, looking as beautiful as ever. "Steven Ross." The crowd had a mixed reaction. There were some cheers, as Steven was a good player on the Parkville High basketball team, which finished in third place in their division. Some parents recognized him from the games, and cheered for him. There were a few boos, mixed in with the claps. Steven was somewhat of a bully in the school. He never put his hands on anyone, but he always tried to make fun of someone that he thought wasn't living by his standards. We were actually cool at this point, but he had to be scared into respecting me.

It was Spring break in Charlotte and in New York City, so Big Tone decided to take a few of his recruitment visits during that week. He was going to visit University of North Carolina at Charlotte for two days, and then go to University of North Carolina at Chapel Hill to see if he could become a member of the Tar Heels. Chapel Hill was his first choice, but he threw the Charlotte visit in just so that he could stay with Moms and me. I hadn't seen Tone since I moved out here, so I knew that I had to have his room, entertainment for the night, and of course some girls to hang out with. There was a Spring Fling party planned at the school gym, so he would have the perfect chance to have a good time there.

Moms picked Tone up from the airport; because I was still fixing up his room and making sure that I had some ladies set up for Tone to hang out with. At about 5pm, I heard Moms' Range Rover pull up in the driveway. I could hear Moms and Tone laughing on their way in. "Anthony, you are crazy boy, no, the Obama family doesn't live in this neighborhood!"

I yelled, "Block Head! What's good Brother? Have you been eating the weights? You got even bigger than when I left you."

Tone gave me a hug. "Country Boy, I missed you, man! Where's my room? I see y'all are doing your thing out there. This is a very good look."

I showed Tone his room. "Get freshened up and take that du rag off, because we are going to a party tonight."

He laughed. "I knew that you wouldn't let me down, Brother. Point to the country girls, and I will follow."

Moms came in the room. "Before you guys go out, tell us how the old neighborhood is doing."

Tone said, "Ma, everybody is hanging in there and just surviving. You know Harlem. Everyday is a day that you worked hard for. Oh yeah, one bit of bad news. Cool Lou was killed last week. He was in a dice game that got robbed on St. Nicholas Avenue. Somebody tried to fight the dude with the gun, and Lou caught a stray bullet to his chest."

Moms hugged me. "That's terrible. I'm so glad we moved out of there. Anthony, I hope that you choose one of these schools down here."

"Yeah, my parents want me to be a Tar Heel, so hopefully this is a good visit." Tone had his license, and surprisingly Moms let him drive the Range Rover to the party. The party was cool; I knew everyone. Dudes were coming over to say what's up and the ladies were all over Tone as soon as we got there.

"Arthur, who is that? He is fine."

"This is what I am talking about, A. You made a name for yourself out here, and you have the ladies lined up for me."

Hector came over to us and said, "What's up Bro? I feel like I know you already, Artie's always talking about you. The way he described you, I thought you would have looked like Ray Lewis from the Ravens!" We all laughed. "Tone, this is my man Hector, a.k.a. Rico Suave. He does his thing with the ladies as well."

Tone shook his hand. "Good to meet you, Man. Are those boots real snakeskin? You're killing them kid." We all laughed.

Jennifer and Steven came over to say hello. Jennifer said, "Nice to meet you, I've heard so much about you. Welcome to Charlotte, this is my boyfriend, Steven." Tone was cool as usual as he hugged Jay Lo, and shook Steve's hand. Then he clapped his big hands, "I see you get a lot of love out here, Artie, but I want to know if anyone out here has been messing with you or making fun of you. Your Big Man is here to take somebody's head off if I need to!" At that moment, Steven and I made eye contact, and he looked helpless. I said, "Na, Tone, I have been given the Southern Hospitality since I've been here."

Tone had a ball that night; he must have danced with at least ten girls. I could swear that he snuck off to the truck with different girls at least once or twice. When I saw him come back in the side door, I asked him to do me a favor.

"Block Head, you see that girl over there on the bleachers reading the book? That's my home girl Stacy. She's very shy, but I want you to introduce yourself, and go dance with her." "I'm on it, A." Tone went into his smooth LL Cool J mode and within two minutes, he got Stacy to dance with him. I couldn't believe this was happening, but it was a good look. It was perfect timing, because Beyonce's song *Love on Top* was playing. That was Stacy's favorite song. While they were dancing, Steven approached me. "Hey Arthur, I know I've been a jerk to you and your friends this year. It would have been easy for you to tell your New York friend about it. I want to thank you, and let you know that I respect you for that. Thank you. You guys have taught me a lot during this school year. Hopefully we can be friends, if you can forgive me for my actions." "It's all good Steve, you are alright with me. Have fun tonight man."

Chapter Nine - S&S

Ms. P grabbed the microphone and said, "Once again, ladies

and gentleman, our valedictorian, Stacy Scott!" The crowd

went crazy. There were cameras flashing, and people clapping

and yelling. Everyone in my section had tears in their eyes.

Stacy Scott. I call her "S&S." (That's the name of a famous D.J

back home.) Stacy is the sweetest, smartest, and even funniest

girl that I know. You would never know, because she has

social phobia. This is a condition that causes her to be terribly

shy in front of crowds or strangers. She is always afraid of

being embarrassed or humiliated. One day, while we were

eating lunch, I asked Stacy, "How did you get to be so shy? I

don't see anything for you to be shy about." Stacy blushed

and said, "Thanks Arthur, when I was five years old, at a

church picnic, I was playing tag with all the other kids. My

foot got caught in a blanket that was in the grass. I tripped

and fell into the picnic table. After I fell and got up off of the

ground, ketchup from the table spilled all over my head. All of the kids and even some of the adults laughed hysterically. I was so heartbroken and embarrassed, that I was never able to do anything in front of a crowd. That's why I always keep to myself and take my time with everything. No one will ever have a reason to laugh at me again."

"Thankfully for me, I sit next to you in class, or I would have never known how great that you are. People are always going to have something to say. What is important is that you know that you are smart, funny, and cute."

Stacy often whispers all of the answers to us in class. She knows all of them, but she is afraid to participate.

One day Ms. P called me into her office, and said, "Arthur, I want you to participate in this year's Scholar Bowl."

I said, "Ms. P, I'm a lot of great things, but a genius is not one of them."

"Stacy Scott has the highest grade point average in the school, and we need her to represent the school at this event. She told me that she would only participate if you were by her side as her teammate."

"I'll do it Ms. P. It will look good on my resume. I do hope they have some fashion, sports or rap questions, though."

The Scholar Bowl is an academic competition between all the schools in the district. We were doing well throughout the competition, because Stacy knew all of the answers. She would whisper to me; then I would ring the buzzer and correctly answer the questions. For the final round, you had to select your Team Captain to come to the circle and face off with the opponent for three final questions. Don't ask me why, but I was selected as Team Captain. Needless to say, without Stacy, second place it was.

I always tried to encourage her, by using a message that my mom gave me. "Stacy, don't ever be too embarrassed to try a new experience. You'll only be putting limits on yourself. You will also be depriving the world of a chance to see S & S in action! Stacy, when you give your best effort in a situation, you cannot lose." She laughed and said, "Thanks, Coach, I'll remember that. Do you want me to tackle the quarterback too?" We both laughed. That was Stacy in a nutshell: she was a genius, but afraid to display her talents. She was very funny. But only her family and I would know that about her.

Stacy has the highest G.P.A in the school. She is the valedictorian and Ms. P told her that she had to give a graduation speech. Last week at the library I said, "S & S, you have to give that speech. You have so many strong points to make. It's a waste for only me to know about it." She said "I really respect the woman that Ms. Palmore is. How strong she is, and how everyone respects her. I spoke to her last week, and she promised to work with me everyday with my speech. I told her that if I am able to practice, and somehow feel comfortable, I will give my speech. I wanted to be strong and fearless, if only for one day. I have been in school with these people for all of these years, and they never heard me say anything meaningful. It will be hard, and I will be anxious, but I think that I am going to give it a try Arthur. I think that you should walk across the stage to get your diploma. I have seen you dance before, and even walk across the room before. Why don't you do it? That would be great." For the first time in a long time, I felt defensive "Na, I'm not going to walk, because the stage is uneven. I could never fall in front of all of those people. I am too cool for that, baby girl."

"No doubts, Party Artie, we both have a lot to think about," she said.

Looking at her walk across the stage with her head held up high has me a little teary eyed. Stacy just reached the whole crowd with her speech earlier in the ceremony. Here is how she ended it. She said. "Friends and fellow graduates, before we head to college or to our future endeavors, let's remember one thing; In order to make it in this world, we have to stand up.

My friends, there come a time in life, when we have to stand up.
We must face our fears head on, and man up.

We must meet our doubts and challenges face to face.
That's how we can do great things and land in a positive place.

Fear is an emotion that mainly comes from within.
If we let it take control, then we can never win.

Being afraid of the dark, can be a time of great fear.
When you finally turn on the light, you see that nothing was there.

Stand up to the bullies that make fun of you.
They are probably jealous of the great things that you can do.

Stand up to the people that say that you can't make it.
When you see an opportunity to succeed, make sure that you
take it.

Stand up to make sure that you are the best that you can be.
If you sit down, then your potential will remain a mystery.

My dear friends please put your right hand up.
Let's make a promise to always Stand Up!

Stacy received a standing ovation from the entire

audience. I am so proud of my friend for overcoming her

fears, for today at least. She received an academic scholarship

to Columbia University.

Chapter Ten- Time to shine

I just turned around to wave at Moms, and right next to her was my friend Alicia Stewart. She is not officially my girl, but we are very close. She is average height, brown skinned, with a short hair cut that we call the Rihanna back home. She had the southern curves, and she was so sweet. My Moms loves her because she is old fashioned and classy, but she is not afraid to put me in my place if necessary. We met at the night of the Spring Fling Dance. Her best friend fell in love with Tone, and we all ended up at the diner after the Party. Alicia goes to Parkville, but she is a junior. Just last week we went to the school prom together.

You already know the Young Prince did it big. I had a Bentley Limo I shared with Hector and his two dates, Jay Lo and Steven, who won the Prom King and Queen, and Stacy, who went solo. I brought a D.J, Superstar Jay from back home, to play the music. My prom had to be right, and he played all of the right songs all night. He had the party rocking all night long. Superstar Jay picked up the microphone and said, "This one is for my main man, Party Artie." He played Jay Z and Alicia Keys' best duet ever, *Empire State of Mind*. He knows that's my all time favorite. I had no choice but to stand up out of my chair and do my famous Party Artie two-step. The whole party tried to do my move, but nobody does it better. We had a great night.

It is almost time for the Young Prince to go to the stage. There go my Moms, my Aunt Rose, and my little cousin Marcus. My Mom told me how proud she is of me for earning a scholarship to the Institute of Art and Design. I want to have my own clothing line one day. It's funny that we moved out here to try to save money for college, but I ended up getting a scholarship after all. Like Moms told me, everything worked out.

My Moms thinks that I should try to walk across the stage to receive my diploma. We spoke about it last week. "Prince, wouldn't it be great if you walked across the stage to get your diploma? We know you can do it, so why don't you show everybody?"

I had to turn down that idea. "Maybe if I had more time to practice or if I was familiar with the stage, I would give it a try. Everyone loves me already, Moms, so no need to give them everything."

"I trust you Son, and you always make the right decision." That was the end of that discussion.

Wow, I can't believe how crazy this year had been. This was a great year, one that will stay with me forever. I met great friends, and had a ton of fun. Hector taught me the value of saving and planning. Jennifer taught me to overcome disabilities and shortcomings by identifying to what I am good at and making the best of my opportunities. Stacy just showed me that when you stand up to your fears, you can do great things. I think I just got the strength that always existed inside of me.

It's my time to shine.

"Arthur Thomas." Principal Palmore called out. Everyone is standing, and cheering. I can feel the heat on my back as I roll up towards the stage. I hear the crowd yelling "Party Artie!" I just got up the ramp to the stage. It feels like Michael Jackson is in the building. Here I go; I am slowly getting up, and I am carefully walking across the stage to accept my diploma. I can see Ms. P crying as I walk towards her. It feels like the auditorium is shaking from all of the crowd movement. I stopped to catch my breath, and when I looked into the crowd, through all of the camera flashes, I saw tears falling down Moms' beautiful face. I accepted my diploma and gave Ms. P a big hug.

Then I grabbed the microphone and said, "Congratulations to the Graduating Class of Parkville High! **STAND UP EVERYBODY!**"

Made in the USA
Charleston, SC
10 October 2012